Pammy the Pig

Written and Illustrated by Pam Fisher

This book is dedicated to all my grandchildren:
Dylan, Molly, Lukas, Jakob and Katie.

Many thanks to Nicole Andriso, Lauri Garbo, Amy Loupin and
Ela Radzyminska for their help with my book.

AuthorHouse™
1663 Liberty Drive
Bloomington, IN 47403
www.authorhouse.com
Phone: 1-800-839-8640

First published by AuthorHouse 2/23/2011
ISBN: 978-1-4567-1796-4 (sc)
Library of Congress Control Number: 2011900082
Printed in the United States of America
This book is printed on acid-free paper.

Because of the dynamic nature of the Internet, any Web addresses or links contained in this book may have changed since publication and may no longer be valid. The views expressed in this work are solely those of the author and do not necessarily reflect the views of the publisher, and the publisher hereby disclaims any responsibility for them.

authorHOUSE®

One beautiful spring day on a farm in Virginia, Patty the pig gave birth to six piglets.

Molly, the farmer's daughter, loved farm animals, especially the new piglets. She thought they were all so cute. She named the piglets Tyler, Aidan, Matt, Amy, David, and Pammy.

Molly noticed that one of the piglets, the one she named Pammy, was smaller than the rest. She also noticed that Pammy's tail did not have a curl like the rest of the piglets.

Patty, Pammy's mother, abandoned Pammy the piglet because she was a little different than the rest of the piglets.

Molly wanted to help Pammy, so she watched over her and bottle fed her just like a real mommy. Molly called all the other farm animals over to the pig pen to see the new piglet.

First, Heather the horse came over to see the new piglet, and she neighed with laughter when she saw Pammy's tail.

Then, Dylan the dog came over to see the new piglet, and he barked with laughter when he saw Pammy's tail.

Lukas the lamb came over to see the new piglet, and he baaed with laughter when he saw Pammy's tail.

When Jake the snake came over to see the new piglet,
he hissed with laughter when he saw Pammy's tail.

Katie the kitten came over to see the new piglet, and she meowed with laughter when she saw Pammy's tail.

Lastly, Lucy the cow came over to see the new piglet, and she mooed with laughter when she saw Pammy's tail.

Pammy became very sad when she saw everyone was laughing at her straight tail. Molly tried to comfort her.

A few days later, Molly was feeding Pammy in the house when they saw a bad storm approaching. All the other farm animals went into the barn for safety.

The sky was black. The wind was blowing so hard that it blew the barn door shut! When the door slammed, the latch came down and locked the door. All the farm animals were locked inside the barn, and they couldn't get out!

When the wind finally stopped blowing, Molly and Pammy went to the barn to check on the farm animals. They tried to get the barn door open, but the latch stayed down keeping it locked.

Molly was worried. How was she going to get the barn door unlocked? How could she get the animals out of the barn?

Molly had an idea! She saw a crack in the barn door that might work. She lifted Pammy and put her straight tail into the crack like a key. Because her tail was so straight, her tail was able to lift up the latch and open the door!

All the farm animals cheered for Pammy! Her straight tail had saved all the animals, and Pammy's mother was so proud of her! Now all the animals were glad that Pammy had a straight tail!

CPSIA information can be obtained
at www.ICGtesting.com
Printed in the USA
250547LV00001B